MW00908374

Bugs In Shoes

Beth Wilder

4880 Lower Valley Road, Atglen, Pennsylvania 19310

Other Schiffer Book By The Author:

The Twilight Realm, A Tarot of Faery
ISBN: 978-0-7643-3393-4 $34.99

all text and images by Beth Wilder

Library of Congress Control Number: 2011941352

Designed by Mark David Bowyer
Type set in Boopee

ISBN: 978-0-7643-3967-7
Printed in China

Schiffer Books are available at special discounts for bulk purchases for sales promotions or premiums. Special editions, including personalized covers, corporate imprints, and excerpts can be created in large quantities for special needs. For more information contact the publisher:

Published by Schiffer Publishing Ltd.
4880 Lower Valley Road
Atglen, PA 19310
Phone: (610) 593-1777; Fax: (610) 593-2002
E-mail: Info@schifferbooks.com

For the largest selection of fine reference books on this and related subjects, please visit our website at **www.schifferbooks.com**
We are always looking for people to write books on new and related subjects. If you have an idea for a book, please contact us at proposals@schifferbooks.com

This book may be purchased from the publisher.
Include $5.00 for shipping.
Please try your bookstore first.
You may write for a free catalog.

In Europe, Schiffer books are distributed by
Bushwood Books
6 Marksbury Ave.
Kew Gardens
Surrey TW9 4JF England
Phone: 44 (0) 20 8392 8585; Fax: 44 (0) 20 8392 9876
E-mail: info@bushwoodbooks.co.uk
Website: www.bushwoodbooks.co.uk

Dedication

Bugs In Shoes is dedicated
to Will, who wanted his very own book,
and Hilary, who wanted to share it
with the world.

Bugs in sneakers

Bugs in heels

Bugs in sandals

Bugs on wheels

Bugs in slippers

Bugs in boots

Bugs in tap shoes

Bugs in suits

Bugs in shorts

Bugs in shirts

Bugs in pants

Bugs in skirts

Bugs in ties

Bugs in socks

Bugs in bows

Bugs in frocks

Bugs in earmuffs

Bugs in coats

Bugs in swimsuits

Bugs in floats

Bugs in ponchos

Bugs in slickers

Bugs in hats

Bugs in knickers

Bugs in house shoes

Bugs in red

Bugs in pajamas

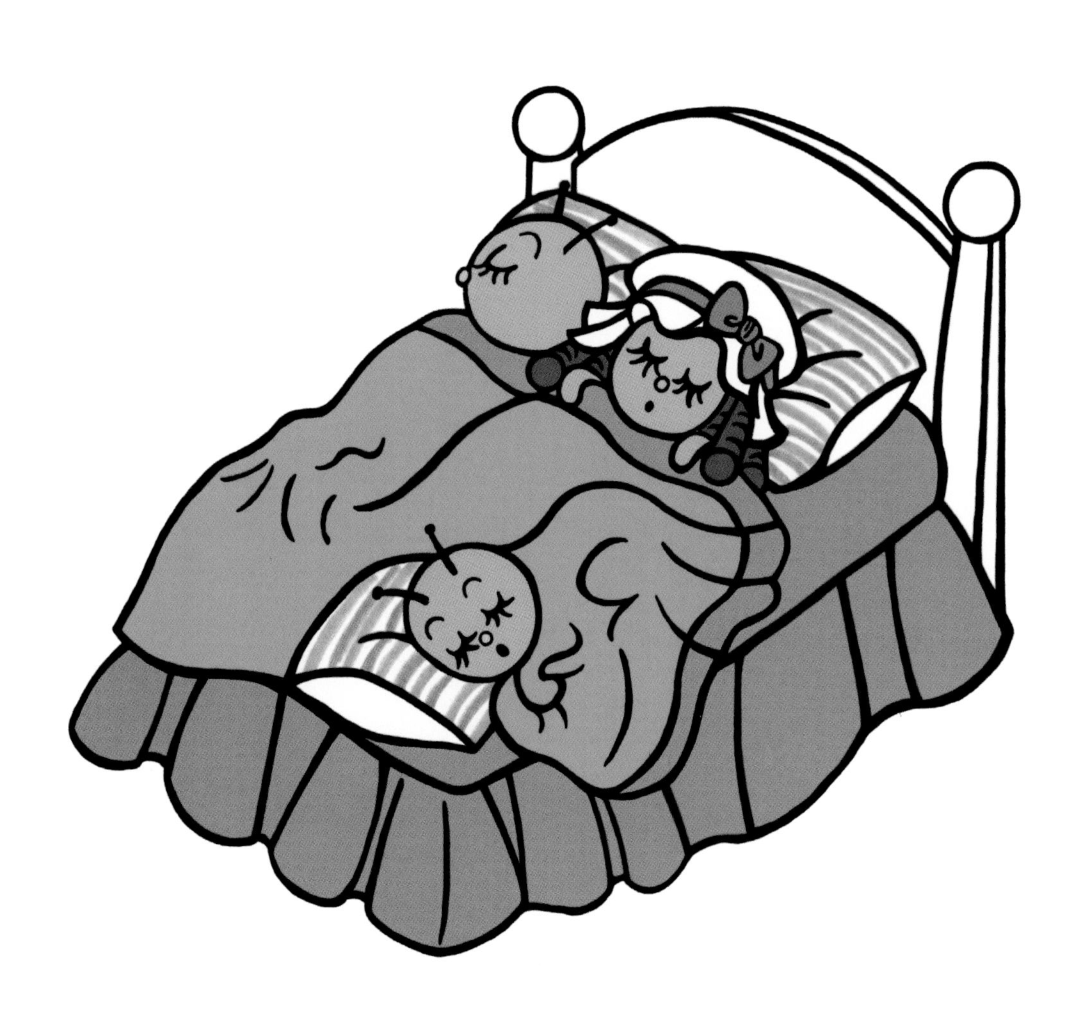

Bugs in bed

Note to Parents

Dear Parents,

Bugs In Shoes was designed to be simple enough for children to pick up easily on the sing-song cadence of the poem and associate the pictures with the words on each page, thus teaching them about different articles of clothing. Hopefully, they will also be able to quickly learn how to read it on their own.

As a child, however, one of my favorite things to do was to crawl up next to my mother as she read bedtime stories to my sisters and me. It is my great hope that you will take time and enjoy reading *Bugs In Shoes* with your children, and that your togetherness will create many happy memories for them.

The following pages can be used as coloring pages and/or photocopied for your children's individual enjoyment.